Disney

THE
LION KING

Ladybird books are widely available, but in case of difficulty may be ordered by post or telephone from:
Ladybird Books – Cash Sales Department Littlegate Road Paignton Devon TQ3 3BE Telephone 0803 554761

A catalogue record for this book is available from the British Library

Published by Ladybird Books Ltd Loughborough Leicestershire UK
LADYBIRD and the device of a Ladybird are trademarks of Ladybird Books Ltd

Disney

THE
LION KING

Ladybird

CHAPTER ONE

The moon had vanished. One by one, each star faded from the cold night sky. Behind the dark eastern hills, the sun rose, turning the flat-topped acacia trees from black to green. Once again, it was dawn on the African plain.

This was an important day.

"Hurry," the animals urged one another. "Today's the day we go to Pride Rock. We can't be late!"

Up from the wide valleys and down from the hills, they paraded across the plain. Cheetahs, the fastest of all, led the way. The dusty ground shook beneath a million drumming hooves and the plodding feet of the elephants and the rhinos. Silent giraffes, followed by their gangly babies, loped alongside herds of excited zebra. At the rear, troops of chattering baboons carried their alert youngsters on their backs.

The air was crowded and noisy with the flap and flutter of countless wings. Birds of all sizes and colours, flying from faraway rivers and trees, shaded the backs of the travelling animals.

The trip was long, and as the animals approached Pride Rock, the plain shimmered

"Here is Simba," said Sarabi, gently handing the spotted cub over to Rafiki. The cub looked up and blinked at the strange old baboon.

Rafiki grinned toothily at Mufasa. "It's as if I'm seeing you as a cub all over again," he said. "Now, little prince, I will give you my blessing." Then Rafiki patted Simba on the head.

Rafiki slowly untied a gourd from his walking stick. He leaned over and shook it several times above the watchful cub. Then he cracked the gourd open, removed some sticky liquid, and smeared it on Simba's forehead. The cub wrinkled his nose.

"Almost finished," the elderly baboon said kindly. He scooped up a handful of dust and sprinkled it over Simba's back. Simba sneezed, and they all laughed.

Then Rafiki stooped down and, with great care, gathered up King Mufasa and Queen Sarabi's son. He carried the cub to the edge of Pride Rock.

The crowd below had been waiting eagerly for this moment.

"There he is," one of them shouted. "Rafiki's holding the new Prince!"

At once all the spectators cheered and stamped their feet.

"Welcome!" they shouted. "Welcome Prince Simba!"

Rafiki waited for the dust to settle. Then he raised Simba high in the air. The clouds parted, and a shaft of sunlight broke through, shining down on the future King. The animals fell silent and bowed.

Rafiki slowly lowered his arms and took Simba back out of sight.

As the afternoon sun began its descent in the western sky, the animals turned to make their way home.

Later that afternoon, Zazu flew to a shaded part of Pride Rock and landed at the feet of another lion — the King's younger brother — Scar.

"It gives me great pleasure to announce the visit of King Mufasa," said Zazu. "And you'd better have a good excuse for missing this morning's ceremony."

"Oooh, I quiver with fear," said Scar calmly.

"What was that?" asked Mufasa, suddenly appearing. "Sarabi and I didn't see you at the presentation of Simba. Is anything wrong?"

"That was *today*?" asked Scar, pretending to be disappointed. "Oh, I feel simply *awful*. Must have slipped my mind."

"You should have been first in line," scolded Zazu. "After all, you are the King's brother."

"I *was* first in line – until the little hairball was born," Scar snorted as he began to walk away.

"Don't turn your back on me, Scar!" ordered Mufasa.

Scar spun round and faced his brother.

"Oh no, Mufasa," he growled. "Perhaps *you* shouldn't turn your back on *me*."

"Is that a challenge?" demanded Mufasa.

Without answering, Scar quickly retreated.

Zazu tried to ease his master's frustration. "There's one in every family, sire," he said, "and they always manage to ruin special occasions."

"What am I going to do with him?" Mufasa muttered under his breath.

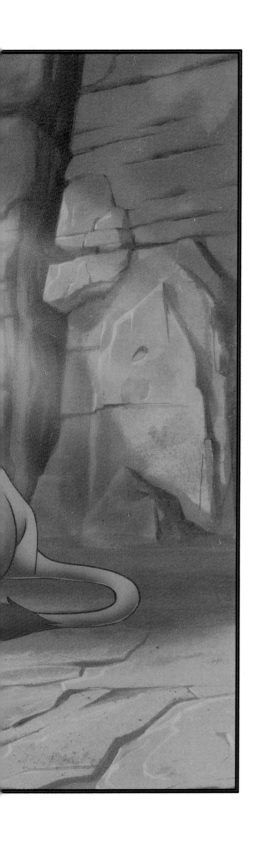

CHAPTER TWO

The days passed quickly for Simba. There was so much to learn and to do. One morning before sunrise, when it was still dark and chilly, he trotted over to his sleeping father and gently nudged him.

"Father," he whispered eagerly into Mufasa's ear.

No answer.

Simba spoke a little louder. "Hey, Father! Wake up!"

Mufasa sighed in his sleep and turned over.

"Father-Father," Simba pressed.

Sarabi sleepily opened her eyes.

"Your son is awake," she said to her mate.

"Before sunrise, he's *your* son," Mufasa grumbled.

Sarabi nudged him hard. "You told him to get you up early this morning."

Mufasa's eyes popped open. "I know. I'm up. I'm up."

Sarabi reached out, pulled Simba close to her, and licked his face and ears.

"Your father has some important things to tell you today," she said. "So you'd better have clean ears."

15

"Mo-ther," said Simba impatiently, wriggling free.

In the dim light Mufasa and Simba strolled far across the Pride Lands. All over the plain, dainty tan-and-white gazelles flicked their tails and nibbled busily on the grass. As Mufasa and Simba passed by, they scattered, leaping stiff-legged and kicking their heels behind them.

A glowing orange ball appeared on the eastern horizon. The sun was beginning a new day. Its heat burned away the morning mist, and Simba felt the ground warming beneath his feet. The sun's long rays reached far out, sweeping across the plain, bringing light to the land.

"Look at the rays of the rising sun, Simba," the King told him. "Everything the light touches is our kingdom."

Simba was impressed. "That's just about everywhere!"

"A king's time as ruler rises and falls like the sun," his father said. "One day the sun will set on my time here. It will rise with you as the new King."

"And all this land will be mine?" asked Simba.

"All of it," said Mufasa.

Simba blinked and scanned the bright plain. Nearby, small, agile mongooses popped in and out of abandoned termite mounds. Out along the sunny horizon, thirsty zebras slowly walked in single file to a crowded watering hole. But far to Simba's left, the land was hazy and still.

"What about that shadowy place?" he asked.

"That's beyond our borders," said Mufasa. "You must *never* go there, my son."

Simba tried not to act disappointed. "But I thought a king could do whatever he wanted."

His father smiled. "There's more to being a king than getting your own way all the time."

"Do you think I'll be a good king, Father?" Simba asked.

Mufasa grew serious and looked into his son's eyes. "You will be a good king if you remember this: everything you see exists together in a delicate balance. As the King you need to understand and preserve that balance. You must respect all creatures — from the crawling ant to the leaping antelope."

"But we *eat* the antelope!" said Simba.

"Yes, we do," said Mufasa. "Let me explain. When we die, our bodies become the grass. Then the antelope eat the grass. And so we are all connected in the great Circle of Life."

"Good morning, sire!" a voice squawked suddenly. It was Zazu. The hornbill landed in a heap at the King's feet. "I have the morning report."

"All right, Zazu," said Mufasa. "Let's hear it."

Zazu cleared his throat and began to speak in his official voice: "The buzz from the bees is that the leopards are in a bit of a spot and..."

Simba was bored. A butterfly flew past him and settled on a flower. The cub pounced, and the butterfly quickly flew away.

While Zazu droned on, Mufasa bent over and whispered to Simba. "What are you doing, son?" he asked.

"Pouncing," said Simba. "But I missed."

Zazu paused and waited.

"Go on, Zazu," said Mufasa.

Zazu continued. "The baboons are going ape. Of course, the giraffes are acting like they're above it all and..."

"Let an old pro show you how to do it," Mufasa said quietly to Simba while Zazu recited his report. "Zazu, would you turn around please?"

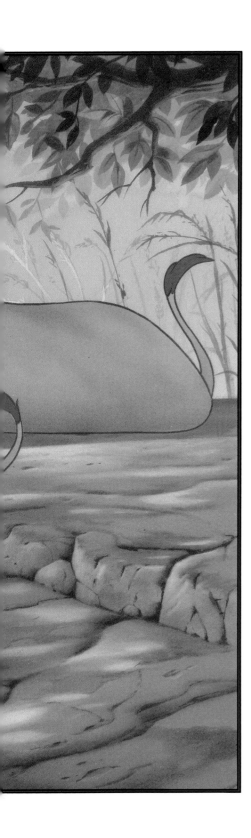

CHAPTER THREE

Simba played with Nala almost every day. They climbed trees together, wrestled and raced across the plain. He couldn't wait to tell her about the elephant graveyard!

He found Nala and her mother, Sarafini, resting in the shade under some trees with Queen Sarabi. Sarafina was giving her impatient daughter a bath.

"Hold still – *please*, Nala," she scolded. "Just a few more licks and you can go."

"Hi, everybody," said Simba.

"How was your walk?" Sarabi asked her son, when he had come closer.

"Fine," said Simba. "Father had to go and check on some hyenas. They've come onto our lands."

Sarabi was startled. "Really? Those hyenas are nothing but trouble!"

"Can Nala and I still go and play?" Simba asked.

Sarafina looked at Sarabi. "Do you think it's safe," she asked, "with the hyenas about?"

"Well," said Sarabi, "it's all right with me as long as Zazu goes with them."

Simba's shoulders slumped. "Please, Mother," he begged. "Can't we go alone?"

"Not today," said Sarabi. "Zazu," she called. "I'd like you to keep an eye on Simba and Nala this afternoon."

Zazu blinked. He was *supposed* to be off duty! With a resigned sigh, he flew down to Simba and Nala.

"Step lively," he said. "The sooner we go, the sooner we come back."

"Yeah," Simba said. "We'll run on ahead."

The two cubs scampered out onto the plain, talking and giggling.

"Where are we going?" asked Nala.

"An elephant graveyard," answered Simba.

Nala's eyes grew big. "Really?" she asked.

"Shh," said Simba, slowing down and whispering. "Zazu!"

"Right," Nala nodded. "How are we going to lose him?"

Zazu fluttered above them. "Just look at you two, telling secrets," he said. "It's so perfect, since you're betrothed and all."

"Be-*what*?" asked Simba. "What's that?"

"You and Nala are betrothed," Zazu sang out. "Intended! Affianced! It means," he explained, "that one day you two are going to be married!"

"I can't marry Nala," Simba protested. "She's my best friend."

"Right!" agreed Nala. "We don't want to get *married*!"

"Sorry to burst your bubble," said Zazu, "but you two turtledoves have no choice. It's all been settled by your parents. It's an old tradition that goes back generations."

"Well, we'll just see," said Simba. "When I'm the King that'll be the first tradition to go. Come on, Nala, I'll race you to that big termite mound."

The two cubs dashed away.

"Oh dear, they're off again," said Zazu, sighing. "Wait for me!"

CHAPTER FIVE

Still running hard, Simba glanced back over his shoulder. Good! No one in sight.

"We made it!" he shouted to Nala. "We made it, Zazu! Zazu? Nala, where's Zazu?"

Nala stopped to catch her breath. She cocked her head and listened.

"Can you hear that?" she asked. "The hyenas are laughing hysterically – maybe they've caught Zazu!"

"We'd better go see!" said Simba.

"No need for that," said Shenzi, suddenly appearing. "We're right – HERE!" Ed was just behind her, giggling.

"Simba!" Nala screamed.

Simba took a hard swipe at Shenzi, forcing her back. "RUN, NALA!" he yelled.

As the two cubs raced back towards the graveyard, Simba spotted an enormous pile of bones.

"Quick," he said. "Let's try to climb over it."

As they scrambled up the pile, Banzai's head poked out from between the elephant bones. "BOO!" he said.

Simba and Nala backtracked in a hurry and bumped right into Shenzi and Ed. There was no escape!

"You two going somewhere?" asked Shenzi.

The cubs skittered between her legs and dashed up another pile of bones.

"Watch out," Simba warned Nala. "It's really shaky up here."

Just as he spoke, they both lost their footing and fell.

Nala gasped — they'd landed inside a giant rib cage.

"We're trapped!" she said to Simba.

Shenzi and Banzai, giggling, sauntered up to them.

"How convenient, Banzai," said Shenzi. "Which snack do you want?"

Simba felt his heart beating wildly. Maybe he could frighten them with a roar. After all, he'd heard his father do it often enough. He took a deep breath.

"Rrrr," he squeaked.

The three hyenas burst into frenzied laughter.

"What was that?" said Shenzi. "Come on, do it again. Come on, kitty, kitty, kitty," she taunted.

Simba took another deep breath.

"ROAAARRRR!"

The three hyenas spun round — and looked straight into the furious eyes of a huge lion.

"It's King Mufasa!" gasped Shenzi. "Quick, guys!" she said to Banzai and Ed. "Let's get out of here!"

Mufasa roared again, and the hyenas fled, howling, into the mist.

"Father," Simba said, trying not to cry, "am I glad to see *you!*"

"You have disobeyed me," Mufasa growled.

Simba had never heard his father sound so angry.

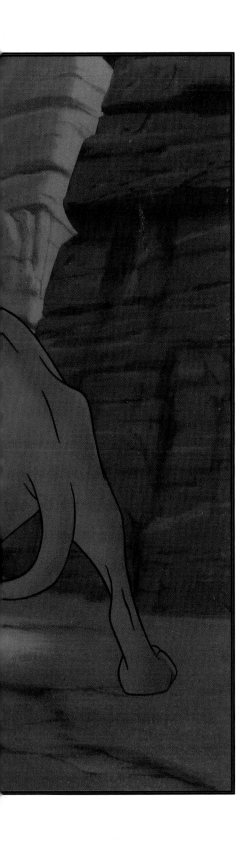

CHAPTER SIX

Next morning Simba followed Scar to the bottom of a wide, deep gorge. The cub cautiously picked his way down the jagged rocks. Every now and then, he tripped.

"Careful, my little one," Scar said sweetly. "We don't want you to fall, do we!"

"Where are we going, Uncle Scar?" asked Simba.

Scar didn't answer. When they reached the bottom he led his nephew to a flat rock in the middle of the gorge.

"Hop up!" he said, gently pushing Simba onto the rock. "Wait here. Your father has a marvellous surprise for you." He turned to leave. "I'll just go tell him that you're ready."

Simba was restless. "I'll go with you!"

"Stay on the rock," Scar insisted. "You don't want to disobey your father and end up in another mess like you did yesterday – with the hyenas."

"You know about that?" asked Simba.

"Simba, my boy," replied Scar, "*everyone* knows about it."

He loped away and left his nephew all alone.

Simba waited patiently. He could hear the

41

mournful grunting sounds of wildebeest in the distance. After a few minutes he noticed a large herd of them moving along the top of the ridge. He sighed. What was keeping his father?

*   *   *

Shenzi, Banzai and Ed waited for Scar's signal.

"Where is Scar?" Banzai asked, peering down into the gorge. "I'm so hungry, I've just gotta have a wildebeest. They're coming this way. If he doesn't hurry, they'll be gone. The whole plan will fall apart."

"You know we have to wait until Scar gives us the sign," said Shenzi. "*Then* we can make our move.

"Look!" she yelped. "There's Scar. There's the signal—let's go!"

Whooping wildly, the hyenas chased after the unsuspecting wildebeest, nipping sharply at their heels. The startled animals bellowed and began to stampede.

"Drive them down into the gorge!" Shenzi yelled to her comrades.

"What do you think I'm trying to do?" coughed Banzai, spitting out dust.

A few minutes later Ed laughed hysterically as the herd veered towards the rim of the gorge.

"There they go!" howled Banzai. "We did it!"

At that moment Mufasa was taking his usual stroll along the top of the gorge. Zazu, perched on his master's back, was reporting the news of the day.

"Look, sire," he pointed out with one of his wings. "The herd is on the move. They're coming this way."

"That's odd," noted Mufasa. As he watched the frenzied wildebeest, his brother, Scar, ran up to him.

"Mufasa!" he shouted. "Quick! A stampede! Simba's down there!"

"I'll fly ahead," cried Zazu.

Mufasa lunged towards the edge of the gorge. "Tell my son I'm coming!" he shouted.

*   *   *

Simba watched as the wildebeest poured down the side of the gorge. There were thousands of them – and they were heading right for him! Wildly scrambling down from the rock, he ran for his life.

Before he knew it, the stampede was practically upon him. The noise of the hooves was deafening, and the dust was so thick that Simba could hardly see. But, some distance ahead of him, he could just see the dim outline of an enormous ancient baobab tree. If only he could reach it before he got trampled to death!

Running so fast that he thought his heart would burst, Simba reached the baobab and clawed his way up the ribbed trunk. He crawled out onto a wide, sturdy-looking limb.

"Simba!" squawked Zazu. He flew through the blinding dust and landed on top of the tree. "Hold on – your father's on his way!"

Simba leaned back to see Zazu. As he shifted his weight, the limb creaked and started to break off.

"Zazu!" screamed Simba. "Help me!"

Zazu squinted through the dusty air and saw Mufasa battling his way through the herd of wildebeest.

"He's over here, sire!" he shouted.

SNAP! The old limb broke, and Simba fell to the hard ground. Mufasa grabbed his son in his mouth. Dodging through the stampeding

animals, he managed to get Simba up onto a rocky ledge on the side of the gorge.

"Oh Father," sobbed Simba. "You came just in time."

Suddenly a galloping wildebeest knocked Mufasa from the ledge. The King fell backwards and was swept away by the stampede.

"Father!" cried Simba. "Father!"

*　　*　　*

Several minutes later, Mufasa managed to pull himself up towards the top of the gorge. Injured and in pain, he clung to an overhanging rock. Slowly he looked up to see his brother poised above him.

"Scar – help me!" he cried.

Scar leaned over and dug his claws into Mufasa's front legs. Then, with a deadly push, he whispered, "Long live the King."

Mufasa crashed down the steep, jagged incline and was still.

Scar looked down from the rim of the gorge and grinned. One down and one to go. It was too bad that Mufasa had rescued Simba, but his nephew would be taken care of soon enough.

He squinted. Was that the little fellow now? It was. Simba was running across the bottom of the gorge. He'd spotted Mufasa lying in the trampled dirt.

By the time Scar reached him, Simba was sobbing next to the dead King.

"Father," whimpered Simba. He buried his face in his father's dusty mane.

"Simba," demanded Scar, "what have *you* done?"

"It was an accident," Simba wailed. "He came to save me."

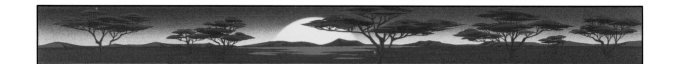

Scar shook his head sadly. "If it weren't for you, he'd still be alive."

"But I didn't mean it, Uncle Scar," said Simba.

"Of course you didn't," said Scar. "No one ever means these things to happen. But the King is dead. And you can *never* show your face in the Pride again."

Simba looked up, wide-eyed. "What am I going to do?"

"Run away, Simba!" said Scar. "Run away and *never* return!"

He watched his nephew run, sobbing, down the length of the gorge. Shenzi and Banzai ambled up behind Scar.

"Nice work," said Banzai. "You got rid of him."

"Now finish the job," ordered Scar, still staring after Simba. "Kill him – now!"

*   *   *

Scar strode triumphantly to Pride Rock. As soon as he arrived he called Sarabi and Zazu to appear before him.

"I have dreadful news," he told them. "My dear brother, Mufasa, and my cherished nephew, Simba, are dead."

"No... no..." moaned Sarabi.

Zazu was too stunned to speak. He tried to pull himself together to console the Queen.

"I'm so sorry," he said gently. "Is there anything I can do for you?"

But the weight of the news had crushed Sarabi, and she slowly sank to the ground.

"You must take comfort that your husband died a hero," said Scar. "It is with a heavy heart that I assume the throne. However, we must never forget the great Mufasa and his beloved son."

The lionesses of Pride Rock heard Sarabi's cry of grief, and they rushed to her side. When they learned the news, their wails echoed across the plain.

By nightfall, thousands of animals had journeyed to Pride Rock. Their last visit had been one of joy to welcome the new Prince. This time they came in grief, mourning his death and that of his father.

Standing on a high ridge, Rafiki sadly shook his head. Then, brokenhearted, the old baboon wandered off to be alone.

CHAPTER SEVEN

Simba stumbled across the dry grass. Thank goodness the hyenas had stopped chasing him! They had turned back after getting stuck in a mass of thornbushes.

But before the hyenas had gone, Simba had heard them scream, "If you ever come back – we'll kill you!"

Now Simba was hot, exhausted and very thirsty. If he didn't find some shade and a watering hole soon, he'd pass out. But, really, he didn't care if he lived or died! If it hadn't been for him, his father would still be alive.

Simba took a few more shaky steps. A shadow passed overhead, and he looked up. Above him, six huge vultures were circling slowly. His knees buckled, and he fainted.

The hungry birds descended. Silently they gathered round Simba.

"Eeeeee-yaaaa!" cried a high voice.

A fat brown warthog, with a skinny meerkat perched on his back, charged towards the surprised vultures.

"Eeeeee-yaaaa!" shouted the meerkat again. "Get out! Get out, you stinkin' buzzards!"

The startled vultures scattered, then took off.

51

The meerkat hopped off and tiptoed cautiously over to Simba for a closer look.

"All right, what do we have here?" he said, carefully lifting Simba's limp paw to examine it. Suddenly he dropped it in alarm.

"Good grief," he croaked to the warthog. "It's a *lion*! And he's alive! Run, Pumbaa—but first, wait for me!" He clambered back onto the warthog. "Let's go, go, go!"

But Pumbaa didn't run. Instead he strutted over to take a look for himself.

"Aw, Timon," he snorted, peering down at the cub, "it's just a little lion. He's so cute and all alone. Can we keep him?"

"Pumbaa," Timon whispered in his companion's ear, "we're talking about a lion. Lions eat guys like us!"

"Maybe if he gets to know us, he'll be on our side," suggested Pumbaa.

Timon scratched his head. "Well, havin' a lion around to protect us might not be such a bad idea, after all."

"So we're keepin' him?" asked Pumbaa.

"Of course!" said Timon.

Pumbaa knelt down and scooped Simba up with his snout.

"Easy does it," said Timon. "We've got a long walk ahead of us. Try not to drop him!"

*   *   *

Later that day, Simba opened his eyes and blinked. A warthog and a meerkat were leaning over him.

"Here, open up," said Timon. He poured some water into Simba's dry mouth. "Are you okay?"

"I guess so," answered Simba. He felt much better.

52

"You nearly died," said Pumbaa. "We saved you."

"Thanks for your help," said Simba, "but I have to go now." He got to his feet and started to walk off.

"Where are you going?" asked Timon.

Simba paused "Nowhere," he sighed.

"Pumbaa," Timon said under his breath, "I think our little lion here is depressed. Come back," he called to Simba. "Tell us where you're from."

"It doesn't matter," said Simba. "Nothing matters now."

"Sounds serious," said Timon. "Did you do something bad?"

"Not just bad," said Simba. "Something terrible. But I don't want to talk about it."

"That's all right," said Pumbaa kindly. "You don't have to."

"That's right," said Timon. "Put your past behind you. Forget it. *Hakuna matata!*"

"What?" said Simba.

"*Hakuna matata,*" Timon repeated. "It means no worries, no responsibilities. That's our philosophy."

"Why don't you stay here with us?" asked Pumbaa.

Simba thought it over. Why not? He had nowhere else to go. And it would be nice to have somebody to talk to.

"I will," he said. "Thanks."

He looked around, really seeing the place for the first time. It wasn't anything like the open plain. Here everything was leafy. Tall trees shaded the ground, making it cool under his feet. High in the branches, red-tailed monkeys and noisy parrots searched for fruit and nuts.

"Where are we?" asked Simba.

54

Timon was surprised. "You've never been in the jungle before?" he asked. "Well then, welcome to our humble home." He pushed back a huge, feathery fern next to him.

Simba peeped in. "It's beautiful," he said. "Do you live in there all the time?"

"We live where we want," said Timon. "We do what we want—we lead the good life! By the way, are you hungry?"

"I sure am," said Simba. Things were really looking up!

"Well then," said the meerkat, "we'll find you some grub."

Timon and Pumbaa began carefully searching the jungle floor. Finally, they stopped before a fallen log.

Getting down on his knees, Pumbaa shoved the log with his snout. Timon felt around under it and grinned. "Enough for all of us!" he said.

Timon held something out to Simba. "Here," he offered.

Simba stared at Timon's upturned paw. In it was a squirming, fat, white worm.

"What's that?" he asked, stepping back.

"I told you—a grub," said Timon. "Try one. They're tasty."

Simba wrinkled his nose. "Eeewww."

"Go on," urged Pumbaa. "You'll learn to love them."

Simba took a deep breath. He was really hungry, and there didn't seem to be much of a choice. He picked up a grub and chewed it.

"Well, what do you think?" asked Timon.

"Slimy, yet satisfying," said Simba, surprised at himself.

Timon smiled. "See! You'll love it here in the jungle. Just remember our problem-free philosophy—*hakuna matata!*"

"Right," said Simba. "*Hakuna matata.*"

CHAPTER EIGHT

Days, weeks and months turned into years. Simba had just about grown up. The spots on his coat had faded long ago and a mane was growing round his head and shoulders.

One night he sat with Timon and Pumbaa under the stars. He liked his friends and the jungle well enough, but it wasn't the sort of life he wanted. Something was missing. *Hakuna matata* just wasn't working for him.

"Do you ever think about what those things are up there?" asked Pumbaa.

"I don't think — I know," said Timon matter-of-factly. "They're fireflies stuck in that bluish black thing."

"Oh," said Pumbaa. "I thought they were big balls of gas, millions of miles away. What do you think they are, Simba?"

Simba was lost in his own thoughts, remembering his father's long-ago words:

The great kings of the past look down on us from those stars. They'll always be there to guide you — and so will I.

"Hello, over there," persisted Timon. "Simba, couldn't you just look at the sky for ever?"

Simba didn't answer. He could imagine

what his father would think of him now. He sighed so deeply that his breath scattered a wispy puff of milkweed into the air.

A sudden wind sprang up. It carried the milkweed over the treetops, far out across the plain and into the waiting, outstretched hand of Rafiki, the old mystic.

The wise, old baboon examined the seeds. Then he hobbled into his cave and studied a picture he'd once painted on the wall. It was of a lion cub.

Rafiki broke open a gourd and removed the sticky liquid. He smeared it around the cub's head. Now the painting changed. It was no longer of a cub, but of a lion with a golden mane.

"It is time," Rafiki said, smiling. And he prepared to leave.

*　　*　　*

The next day Pumbaa was helping Timon hunt for bugs. They weren't having much luck.

"We'll find some faster," said Timon, "if we split up. You go this way and I'll go that way."

"I'd rather go that way and you go this way," said Pumbaa. "But if you *really* want to go that way, I can go..."

"Stop!" interrupted Timon. "Just go some way!"

Pumbaa trotted up to a thornbush. Maybe he'd find some ants on it. He sniffed around the prickly branches—just as he'd thought!

"Timon!" he woofed. "Over here!"

He heard a twig break behind him and turned to face his friend. "I found a whole lot of ants."

Pumbaa froze. The hairs bristled on the back of his neck, and his

tail stood up straight. It wasn't Timon, after all. It was a lioness – and she looked hungry.

"*TIMON! HELP!*" he squealed. Frantic, Pumbaa dug himself under a big fallen log and got wedged in halfway.

Timon came running. "Pumbaa?" he asked, looking at his friend's thrashing hind legs. "What are you doing under there?"

"She's gonna eat me!" screamed Pumbaa.

"Who's *she*?" asked Timon. Then he saw the lioness – and she was about to leap straight at him! Terrified, Timon shut his eyes. But nothing happened. He peeped out of one eye just as Simba shot from the bushes and tackled the lioness. They rolled over and over, grunting loudly.

"He's got her!" squealed Timon, skipping about on his hind legs. "Oh no! She's got him. Wow! He's movin' like a champ. See, Pumbaa – I told you he'd come in handy! Get her! Bite her head!"

Suddenly the lioness flipped Simba over on his back, pinning him down with her paw.

Simba looked at her closely. "Nala?"

"Simba?" asked the lioness.

Timon watched in shock as Simba and the newcomer pranced about, roaring in delight.

"Hey, what's goin' on here?" asked Timon.

"Nala, you look great!" said Simba. "What are you doing here?"

"What do you mean, what am *I* doing here?" asked Nala. "I thought you were dead!"

"Nope," said Simba. "Here I am."

"It's so good to see you," said Nala.

60

"I repeat," Timon interrupted, "WHAT'S GOIN' ON HERE?"

"Timon," said Simba, "meet Nala. She's my best friend."

"Friend!" snorted Timon. "She tried to eat us."

"Sorry," said Nala. "I didn't know who you were."

Pumbaa, having just managed to free himself, sat panting on the ground.

"Oh Pumbaa," said Simba, "this is Nala."

Pumbaa tried to catch his breath. "Pleased to meet you."

Nala smiled at the warthog. Then she grew serious. "Simba," she asked, "why would Scar tell us you were dead?"

"It doesn't matter," said Simba. "I'm alive."

"Of course it matters," said Nala. "You're the King."

At once, Pumbaa dropped to his knees. "Your Majesty," he said, "I gravel at your feet."

"Get up," said Timon. "It's not *gravel*. It's *grovel*. And don't. Believe me, he's not *the* King."

"Tell him the truth, Simba," Nala urged him.

"Yeah, she's right," admitted Simba.

"Now everything's ruined!" cried Timon. "It'll never be the same around here."

Nala turned to Timon and Pumbaa. "Would you both excuse us for a little while? I'd like to talk to Simba alone."

"Sure," said Timon in a huff. "Come on, Pumbaa."

"I knew it!" said Pumbaa as they walked away. "I knew he was a king all along."

"Well, I'm surprised!" admitted Timon. "You think you know a guy..."

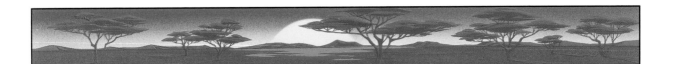

"You never told them who you are?" asked Nala when they were by themselves.

"They never asked," said Simba. "Look, enough about me. How did you get here?"

"Things are terrible at home," said Nala. "Scar has taken over. He lets the hyenas do whatever they want!"

Simba was shocked. "That sounds awful!" he said.

"It got so bad," Nala went on, "that I couldn't take it any more. So I ran away. I guess I thought I'd find something better."

"And you did – me!" said Simba with a big grin. "Now we can have a great life together."

Nala smiled sadly. "It sounds perfect, Simba, but we can't. We're not all that matters. Now that we're together, we can go back to Pride Rock to set things right."

"Nala," Simba tried to explain, "I live by a new philosophy now. *Hakuna matata*. It means no cares, no worries, no responsibilities."

"Listen to me!" interrupted Nala. "Forget this *hakuna matata* business. Accept your responsibilities, Simba. With you alive, Scar has no right to the throne."

Simba shook his head.

"Nala," he persisted, "I just can't go back. I'm no king."

"You could be," Nala told him.

Simba gazed deep into Nala's eyes. "I've missed you, Nala."

"I've missed you, too," Nala said.

"Let me show you round. I'm sure you'll get to like it here," he said. "Come on. *Please*."

Nala followed him into the leafy, sun-dappled jungle.

"It's beautiful," she gasped. "I can see why you like it. This whole place is like a paradise."

"I told you," said Simba, stretching out on a soft bed of moss. "This is all we need."

Nala started to walk away.

"Nala," said Simba, "there's one more place I want to show you. It's one of my favourite spots."

He took her to a little waterfall. The water bounced and sparkled as it fell in a rainbow mist.

Simba jumped into the icy pond. "Come on in!" he called, slapping the water with his paw.

Nala hesitated, then laughed and joined him.

All afternoon they played hide-and-seek in the tumbling falls. When the air grew cool, they strolled to a hilltop and watched the sun set.

"Nala," Simba said, nuzzling her, "stay with me. Why go back to a world that's defeated us?"

Nala looked away. She couldn't bear to hear Simba talk like that. She couldn't believe Mufasa's son would turn his back on the Pride.

"You're hiding from the future, Simba," she answered.

"It's too hard for me to give up what's here," said Simba. "You don't understand."

"Neither would your father. Mufasa would want you to go back," she told him.

Simba blinked back his tears. "My father is dead."

CHAPTER NINE

Simba couldn't sleep. His talk with Nala kept going round and round in his head. He looked over at her. She was sleeping quietly. Maybe a little walk would help to make him drowsy.

The jungle was unusually quiet. Simba strolled for a few minutes, then stretched out on a flat rock and gazed at the sky. It was packed with stars.

I can't go back, he thought. *How could I show my face in the Pride? I'm no king. I can't right the wrongs of the world.*

"And even if I tried," he sighed out loud, "I'm not you, Father. I never will be."

Gradually Simba became aware of a faint sound — the sound of someone singing a strange little tune. *"Asante sana, squash banana. We we nugu, mi mi apana."*

Simba strained to hear the words. He couldn't tell where they were coming from. But something about them was sad and disturbing, so he decided to move on.

In a little while he stopped to rest again. He relaxed along a fallen log that bridged a narrow stream. *PLOPPP!* A stone thrown from the shore had landed in the water, narrowly missing his head.

Startled and annoyed, Simba saw an old baboon squatting by the side of the stream. Rafiki grinned at Simba. *"Asante sana, squash banana. We we nugu, mi mi apana,"* he crooned.

"Are you following me?" asked Simba. "Who are you?"

Rafiki looked him in the eye. "The question is," he replied, "who are *you?*"

Simba sighed. "I thought I knew. Now I'm not so sure."

"Well," said Rafiki, "I do know who you are. You're Mufasa's son. "Bye now," he added, as he scooted away through the undergrowth.

Simba could hardly believe what he'd just heard. The old baboon knew his father? He had to stop him before he got away.

"Wait!" shouted Simba. He charged through the vines and chased Rafiki up to the top of a rocky hill.

"You knew my father?" he asked him.

Rafiki shook his head. "Let me correct you," he said. "I *know* your father."

Simba felt sorry he had to give such bad news to the old baboon. "I hate to tell you this," he said, "but my father died a long time ago."

"Let me correct you again," Rafiki said. "Your father *is* alive! You follow Rafiki. He knows the way."

Simba's heart swelled with hope. Rafiki's name stirred up long-ago memories of Pride Rock. Now, for the first time since he'd left home, he felt truly happy. He was going to see his father again!

The old baboon was surprisingly quick, and it was hard to keep up with him. One second he'd be in sight, and the next he'd be gone, as if by magic. When Simba thought he'd lost track of Rafiki for good, he saw him beckoning.

"Hurry! Don't dawdle!" Rafiki called out. "Mufasa's waiting."

He led the way through more tangles and undergrowth. At last he stopped near a deep pool screened by leafy plants and tall reeds.

"Is my father here?" asked Simba.

Rafiki hobbled up to the reeds and parted them.

"Shh," he murmured, putting a long bony finger to his grey lips. "Look down there."

Simba crept closer and looked into the still pool. The water sparkled with the reflection of the stars. Gazing at him, through the stars, was a lion with a golden mane.

"Father?" asked Simba. As he leaned forward, he realised it wasn't his father at all. He was just looking at himself. Overwhelmed with disappointment, he turned to Rafiki. Was the old baboon playing some kind of cruel trick?

"That's not my father," Simba told him. "It's just my reflection."

"Look harder," said Rafiki.

Puzzled, Simba stared into the shining water again. His reflection shimmered and gradually changed shape. It was turning into Musafa's image!

Simba gasped.

"You see," said Rafiki, "he lives in *you*."

"*Simba...*"

Simba looked up. It was his father's voice!

"Father, where are you?" he cried.

Before Simba's amazed eyes, a swirl of clouds parted, and Mufasa's image slowly filled the night sky. But it wasn't really his father—he could see right through him. Simba gulped. He was looking at a ghost!

"Father?" he asked, beginning to feel afraid.

"Simba, have you forgotten me?" asked Mufasa.

"No!" cried Simba. How could his father ever think that?

The King's image changed again. Simba could no longer see the ghost, but he could feel his father's presence all around him. Mufasa had become part of the air itself.

"You have forgotten who you are," said the voice of Mufasa. *"And so, you have forgotten me."*

"Oh no," insisted Simba. He felt a sob rising in his throat. "I'd never forget you."

Mufasa's voice grew gentle. *"Look inside yourself, Simba. You are more than what you have been. You must take your place in the Circle of Life."*

"But Father, I've made a place for myself here," explained Simba. "I'm not who I used to be. How can I go back?"

"Remember who you are," said his father. *"You are my son and the one true King."*

Mufasa's voice started to fade.

"Remember who you are..."

"Father!" pleaded Simba. "Please don't go! Don't leave me!"

"Remember... remember..." repeated the voice as it faded away.

"Father?" Simba called faintly. But Mufasa was gone, and so was Rafiki. They'd both left him by himself in the dark.

Simba retraced his steps through the jungle. But now he wasn't really alone. He had the stars to guide him.

*　　*　　*

Just before dawn, Nala's voice woke Pumbaa and Timon.

71

"I was calling for Simba," she told them. "Is he here?"

Timon looked surprised. "We thought he was with you."

"Where'd he go?" asked Pumbaa.

"I don't know," explained Nala. "When did you see him last?"

"When he was with you!" said Timon.

"Ha-ha," interrupted Rafiki, squatting on a tree limb above them. "You won't find him here. The King has returned to Pride Rock."

Hearing the old baboon's words, Nala roared in delight. "He's really gone back!" She watched Rafiki quickly disappear into the trees. *I was wrong about Simba*, she thought.

"What's goin' on here?" demanded Timon. "Who's the monkey?"

"Simba's gone back to challenge Scar," said Nala.

"Who's got a scar?" asked Pumbaa.

"No, no, no," said Nala. "It's his uncle."

Timon was amazed. "The monkey's his uncle?"

"No," explained Nala slowly. "Simba's gone back to challenge his uncle, to take his place as the King."

"Ohhhh," said Timon and Pumbaa together.

Timon thought it over. "A challenge?" he asked in a worried voice. "You mean it might be a fight – to the death?"

Nala nodded sadly.

Pumbaa gasped. "Simba might be killed!"

"*You!*" Timon yelled at Nala. "This is because of *you!*"

"You don't understand, Timon," said Nala.

"I don't understand?" squealed Timon. "*You* don't understand. Simba's marchin' off into the jaws of death – and it's *your* fault." He began to sob.

Nala turned to leave.

"Hey," said Timon, looking up. "Where are you goin'?"

"I'm going with Simba," said Nala.

"I'm going, too," said Pumbaa. "Like Simba, who marches off into the face of death, I, too, go to meet my destiny — as his faithful friend."

"Fine!" yelled Timon. "Go! Be a hero. Who needs you here, anyway? Now *I'm* the King of the jungle!"

Timon stood and watched until Nala and Pumbaa were nearly out of sight. Then, all at once, he bolted after them.

"Hey, you guys," he shouted, "wait for me!"

CHAPTER TEN

Simba climbed to the top of a high plateau. At last he'd reached the edge of the Pride Lands. Pride Rock stood tall in the middle of the empty, parched plain.

Everything had been touched by the drought. The trees were almost leafless. Starving giraffes, stretching as high as possible, had eaten the branches bare. The enormous ancient baobabs were stripped, their stringy bark devoured by desperate, hungry elephants.

The dry wind picked up, and threatening clouds gathered overhead. Perhaps they were bringing rain! As the wind blew his mane, Simba breathed deeply and closed his eyes. He thought of his father's words. *Remember... remember...*

Then he went down into the Pride Lands.

*   *   *

Inside Scar's cave, Zazu was locked in a cage, humming mournfully to himself.

"Sing something with a little bounce to it!" Scar ordered.

"I would never be treated like this by Mufasa," said Zazu.

"*What* did you say?" Scar exploded.

75

"You are never *ever* to say that name in my presence. *I* am the King!"

"Yes, sire," Zazu said meekly. Then, more boldly, he said, "Only *you* could rule the Pride as you do."

Just then Shenzi, Banzai and Ed burst into the cave.

"You gotta do something, boss," howled Shenzi. "It's dinner time, and we haven't even got any starters!"

"Yeah – and there's no food, either," cried Banzai.

"The hyenas are so hungry they're ready to riot!" said Shenzi.

"It's the lionesses' job to hunt for food," snarled Scar. "Must I do *everything?*"

He poked his head out of the cave. "Saar-ra-bee!" he roared.

*　　*　　*

A few minutes later Sarabi arrived.

"Listen to all those hungry stomachs out there," Scar told her.

"Scar," said Sarabi, "there's no food – the herds have moved on. We have no choice. We must leave Pride Rock."

"We're not going anywhere," said Scar. "I'm the King, and I make the rules!"

"If you were half the king Mufasa was..." Sarabi began.

"I AM TEN TIMES THE KING MUFASA WAS!" roared Scar, and with a powerful swipe of his paw, he knocked Sarabi to the ground.

The other animals fell silent as lightning flashed in the dark sky. High above the plain, storm clouds began to churn. Thunder boomed. The wind howled and roared. *Zaapp!* A blinding lightning bolt scorched the earth, and the dry grasses caught fire. Swirling flames swept towards Pride Rock.

76

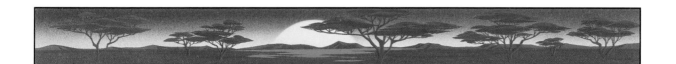

Staring into the smoky air, Scar gasped. Coming like a ghost through the smoky haze was a golden-maned lion.

"Mufasa? No! It can't be!" he said, backing up. "You're dead!"

Sarabi raised her aching head. "Mufasa?" she asked.

"No, Mother," said Simba. "It's me."

"Simba... you're alive," said Sarabi weakly.

"Simba?" whispered Scar. Then he quickly recovered from his shock. "Well, Simba. I'm surprised to see you. Stroke of bad timing, your showing up now."

"I'd say I'm right on time," said Simba.

"Well, you know," Scar stumbled, "the pressures of ruling a kingdom..."

"Are no longer yours," finished Simba. "I've come back to take my place as the King."

"Sorry, Nephew," Scar said. "I would step down, but..."

He turned and signalled to the crowd of starving hyenas. Instantly they swarmed towards Simba. Caught off balance, Simba was pushed backwards, and he slipped over the cliff's edge. Digging his claws into the crumbling earth, he barely held on.

"Enough!" ordered Scar, calling off the hyenas.

He ambled over and looked down at Simba.

"Poor, pathetic Simba," Scar sneered. "Ever since you were a cub, wherever you went, disaster followed."

"Step down, Scar," Simba said, trying desperately to regain his footing.

"Always in the wrong place, aren't you?" Scar continued. "Only this time your father isn't here to save you. In fact, he died trying to save you."

79

Sorrow flooded Simba's heart. Even though his father's death had been an accident, his own guilt was still almost more than he could bear.

"Now *this* looks familiar," Scar continued, grinning maliciously. "Where have I… oh yes, I remember! This is just the way your father looked before *I* killed him!"

The words struck Simba with the force of a blow. Scar had murdered his father! A new strength surged through his body, and with an explosive roar, he lunged upwards, pushing his uncle onto his back.

"Help me, you idiots!" Scar screamed to the hyenas. As they leapt upon Simba, Scar scrambled to his feet.

From the corner of his eye Simba saw Nala spring to his aid. Side by side, the two of them faced the attacking hyenas. And with ear-piercing battle cries the lionesses of Pride Rock joined in. Throughout their terrible fight, the fire roared around the base of Pride Rock, filling the air with choking smoke and ash.

Finally, after the hyenas had fled in defeat, Simba and Scar met face to face.

"Murderer!" Simba cried out.

"Please don't hurt me," begged Scar. He had no one to help him. His back was to the cliff. "I didn't kill your father. It was the hyenas. They're evil, Simba. I'm your family."

Simba paused briefly, considering his uncle's plea. "Run away, Scar," Simba ordered. "Go – and never show your face again."

"Y-yes, Your Majesty. As you wish," Scar said, pretending to leave. Then, snarling, he spun round and struck out at his nephew.

Simba moved quickly. "You've lost your chance!" he roared. He grabbed Scar and heaved him over the edge.

At the bottom of the cliff, the waiting pack of starving hyenas threw themselves upon him. The hyenas' laughter echoed through the rocks. Scar was no longer their master, and within minutes he was no more.

Above, Simba felt someone at his side.

"Welcome home," Nala said. "Your mother is waiting to greet the new King."

Simba nuzzled her. "It's good to be back."

"That was quite a battle," said Nala. "Timon even came to the rescue. He and Pumbaa got rid of Shenzi, Banzai and Ed."

Simba smiled. "And how's Zazu?"

"Fine," Nala quipped. "He's free as a bird!"

As they smiled at each other, it started to rain. The pounding drops put out the fire and soaked the black, smoky ground. Within minutes, sheets of water drenched the plain, and gurgling streams snaked across the land once again.

CHAPTER ELEVEN

The Pride Lands came back to life. The watering holes overflowed, and the grasses grew green and tall. Acacia trees, their branches heavy with tiny golden puffballs, scented the air and the kigelia trees bloomed. At night, when the flowers opened, fruit bats drank the nectar.

One morning at dawn, all the animals journeyed to the foot of Pride Rock. Zazu circled low above them and then flew out of sight.

"Why are we here?" a young zebra asked.

"Be patient," said his father. "Soon you will see the little Prince. Look! There he is now!"

On top of Pride Rock, Timon and Pumbaa sat amid a group of lionesses. They watched as the strange old baboon sprinkled a handful of dust over the little cub's head. The cub sneezed, and everyone laughed.

Rafiki picked up the wriggling cub and moved to the edge. At once everyone cheered and stamped their feet.

Then Rafiki raised the cub — the son of King Simba and Queen Nala — high in the air.

The animals fell silent and bowed to their future king.

   After the crowd had gone, Simba stood at the top of Pride Rock.
He watched the sun set beyond the western hills. It was evening once
again on the African plain.

   "Everything is all right, Father," Simba said softly. "You see, I
remembered." He gazed upwards. One by one, each star took its place
in the cold night sky and seemed to twinkle in reply.